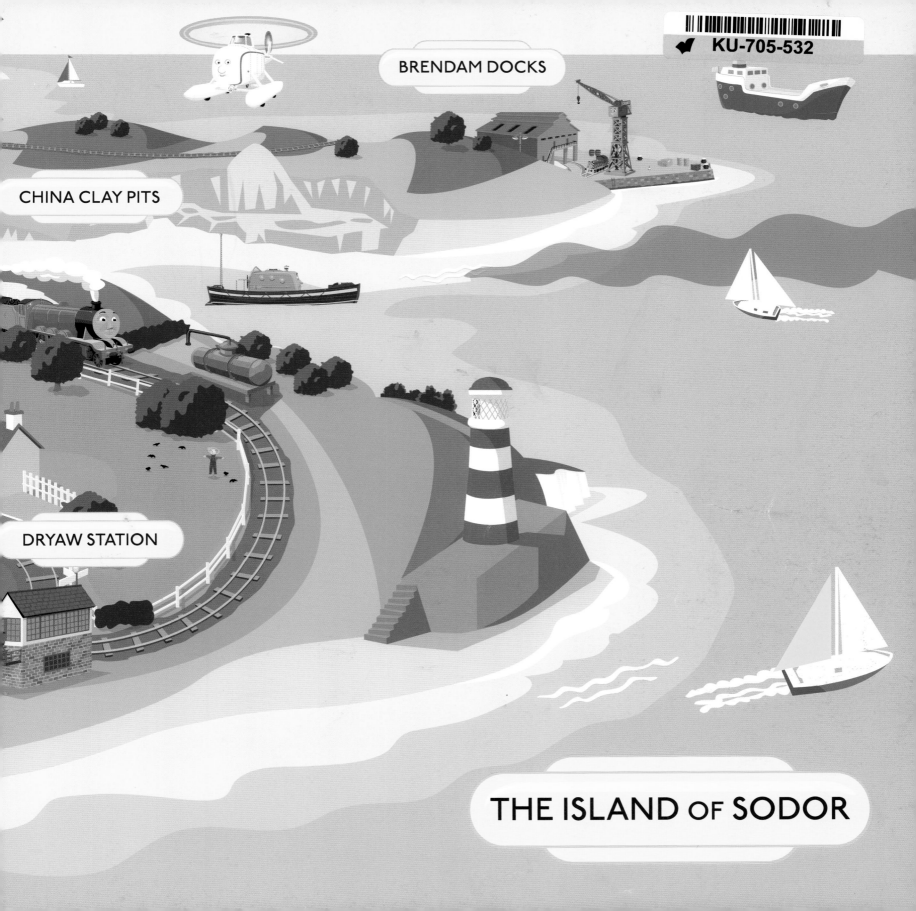

BRENDAM DOCKS

CHINA CLAY PITS

DRYAW STATION

THE ISLAND OF SODOR

First published in Great Britain 2022 by Farshore
An imprint of HarperCollins*Publishers*
1 London Bridge Street
London SE1 9GF
www.farshore.co.uk

HarperCollins*Publishers*
1st Floor, Watermarque Building, Ringsend Road
Dublin 4, Ireland

Written by Laura Jackson
Illustrated by Robin Davies
Map illustration by Dan Crisp

CREATED BY BRITT ALLCROFT

Based on the Railway Series by the Reverend W Awdry
© 2022 Gullane (Thomas) Limited.
Thomas the Tank Engine & Friends ™ and Thomas & Friends ™
are trademarks of Gullane (Thomas) Limited.
© 2022 HIT Entertainment Limited. HIT and the HIT logo are
trademarks of HIT Entertainment Limited.

ISBN 978 0 7555 0413 8
Printed in United Kingdom
001

A CIP catalogue record for this title is available from the British Library.

MIX
Paper from
responsible sources
FSC™ C007454

This book is produced from independently certified FSC™ paper
to ensure responsible forest management.

For more information visit: www.harpercollins.co.uk/green

This book
belongs to

....

....

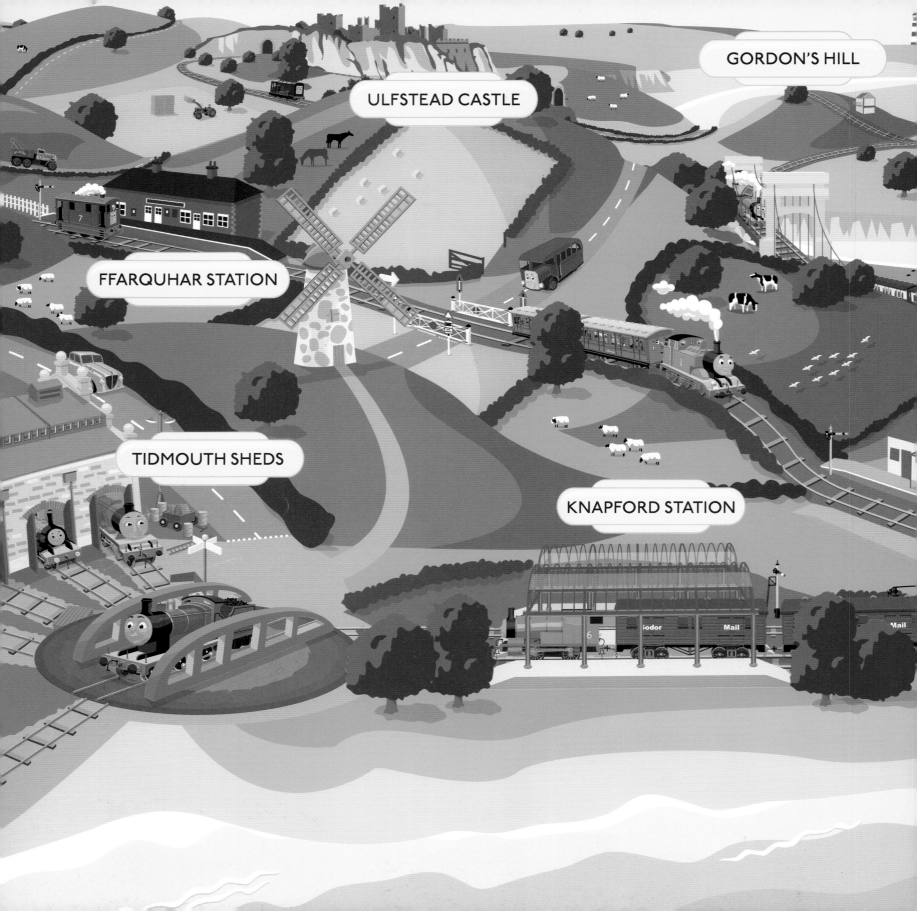

GORDON'S HILL

ULFSTEAD CASTLE

FFARQUHAR STATION

TIDMOUTH SHEDS

KNAPFORD STATION

Thomas goes on Holiday

This is the story of Thomas, the adventurous blue engine, and the time he went on a grand holiday around Great Britain …

One sunny morning on Sodor, Thomas was getting ready for a very important job.

He was going on a tour of Great Britain.

"You will pick up passengers in **Edinburgh** and take them on holiday to **Brighton,"** said Sir Topham Hatt. "A tour guide will show you the stops on the way."

Wheeeeessh!

Thomas was so excited.

After a long journey, Thomas arrived at his first stop.

"Welcome to Edinburgh!" said the tour guide. She pointed to a big, spooky-looking building. "Did you know Edinburgh Castle is nearly 900 years old?"

"That's nearly as old as Gordon," giggled Thomas.

In no time at all, the passengers and the luggage were on board. Thomas was ready to roll!

"Whee! I'm Thomas on Tour!" Thomas whistled to a shiny, fast train.
Whooosh! The train sped past.

"No stopping ahead. No stopping ahead," warned the tour guide.

But Thomas wasn't listening. He had seen something standing in
a field. Something *huge* ...

Clickety-clack, clickety-clack! Thomas steamed through the Scottish countryside.

Faster, faster, faster! Thomas zoomed into England.

Screeech! Thomas skidded to a stop.

Bump! All the luggage tumbled onto the tracks.

"Oh no! Sorry!" puffed Thomas. **"B-b-but ... g-g-giant!"**

Thomas stared at a big shape ahead.

"That's a sculpture, Thomas," said the tour guide.
"It's the **Angel of the North.**"

Thomas blushed. He had made a big mess on
the tracks! But help soon arrived to clear
the luggage.

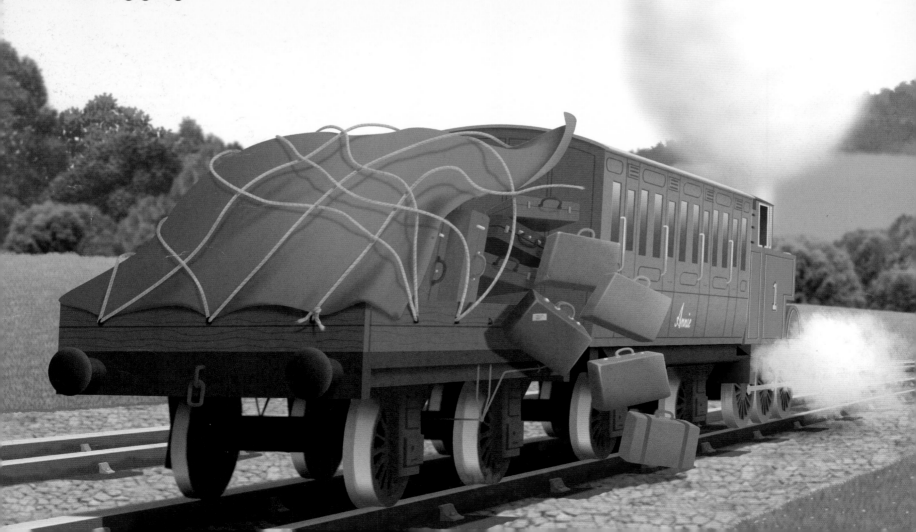

It was dark when Thomas rolled up to his last stop for the night. A big, bright light was twinkling in the sky.

"Wow! Look at that tall star!" gasped Thomas.

The tour guide smiled. "That's not a star, it's **The Blackpool Tower.**"

Thomas thought the twinkly tower was **amazing.**

Early the next morning, the station guard woke Thomas.

"Time to collect more coal!" he said.

But Thomas was so tired.

"I'll just have a bit more sleep ..." he yawned.

When he woke up again, the passengers were all climbing on board.

"Next stop, Snowdonia!" called the tour guide.

Thomas was so excited, he forgot all about the coal.

Whirr! Whirr! Whirr! Thomas was soon whizzing through Wales. He steamed past Conwy Castle …

… and he saw Mount Snowdon. Thomas was excited! He was so excited, he didn't notice his engine starting to fizz …

… and his wheels turning slower, slower, slower. **Screech!** Thomas suddenly flew back down the track and came to a stop.

He had completely run out of coal. Oh dear.
Poor Thomas didn't feel like a Useful Engine at all.

After Thomas was filled up with coal the next day, he was determined to be a **Really Useful Engine.**

"Stay on the branch line to London," the tour guide called out.

But Thomas had another idea. The main line was faster than the branch line.

"I'll switch tracks, then I'll be **super-duper speedy!**" thought Thomas.

But the main line wasn't fast at all.

The main line was **bumpy** and **broken**. A big sign blocked the way. The track ahead was closed for repairs.

"Fizzling Fireboxes! I should have stayed on the branch line," puffed Thomas. "I should have listened ..."

Thomas slowly bumped back up the track. "Maybe if I just listen more, I can be **useful** again?" he thought.

Sure enough, back on the branch line Thomas **whizzed** to London bang on time.

A friendly barge called Dilly showed Thomas the sights. He listened to everything she said.

"There's Big Ben," Dilly said about a clock tower. "Big Ben is the nickname for the clock's bell."

"Woah," peeped Thomas. "Listening is **fun** and I like learning new things too!"

Then when the tour guide told Thomas to travel slowly to **Brighton,** he listened. He **chugged** steadily on his muddy wheels.

Thomas was dirty, tired and needed repairs, but as he pulled into Brighton station, he was **happy** to be **useful** again.

"Hurrah for Thomas the Tour Engine!" all the passengers cheered.

After a washdown, his buffers were buffed and he was fitted with **shiny** new wheels.

"Now you can have a holiday too, Thomas!" smiled the tour guide.

Thomas giggled. He had no problem listening this time. He was definitely ready to have a **Very Useful** holiday of his own.

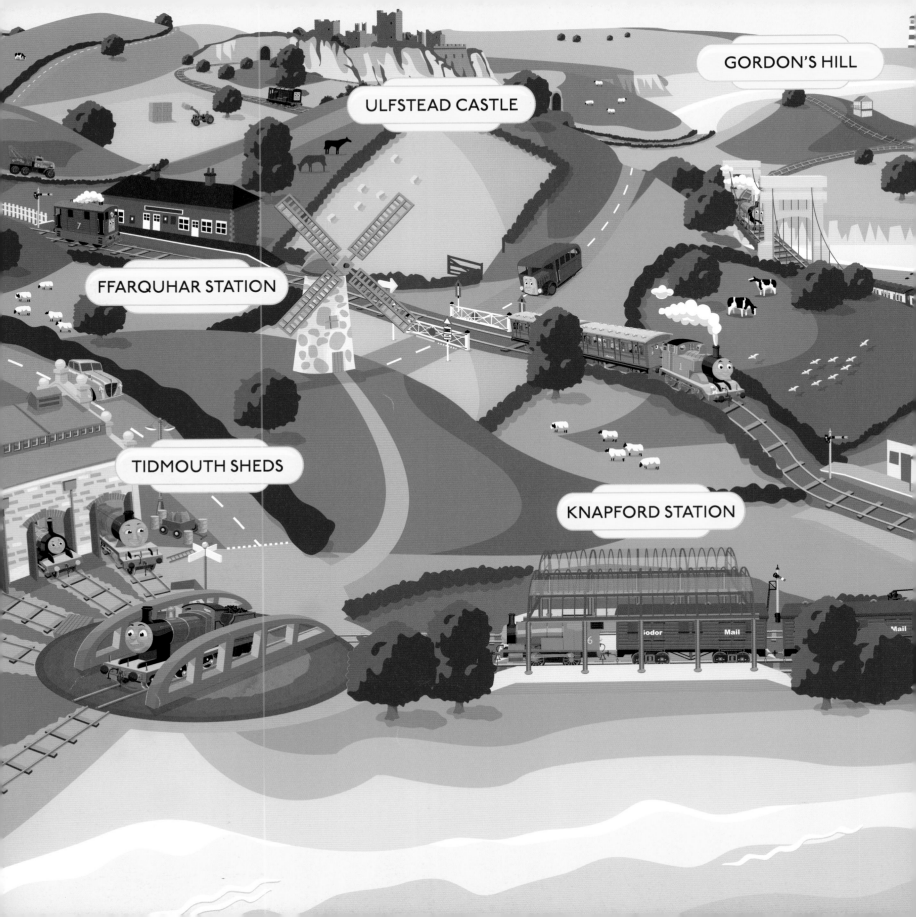

GORDON'S HILL

ULFSTEAD CASTLE

FFARQUHAR STATION

TIDMOUTH SHEDS

KNAPFORD STATION

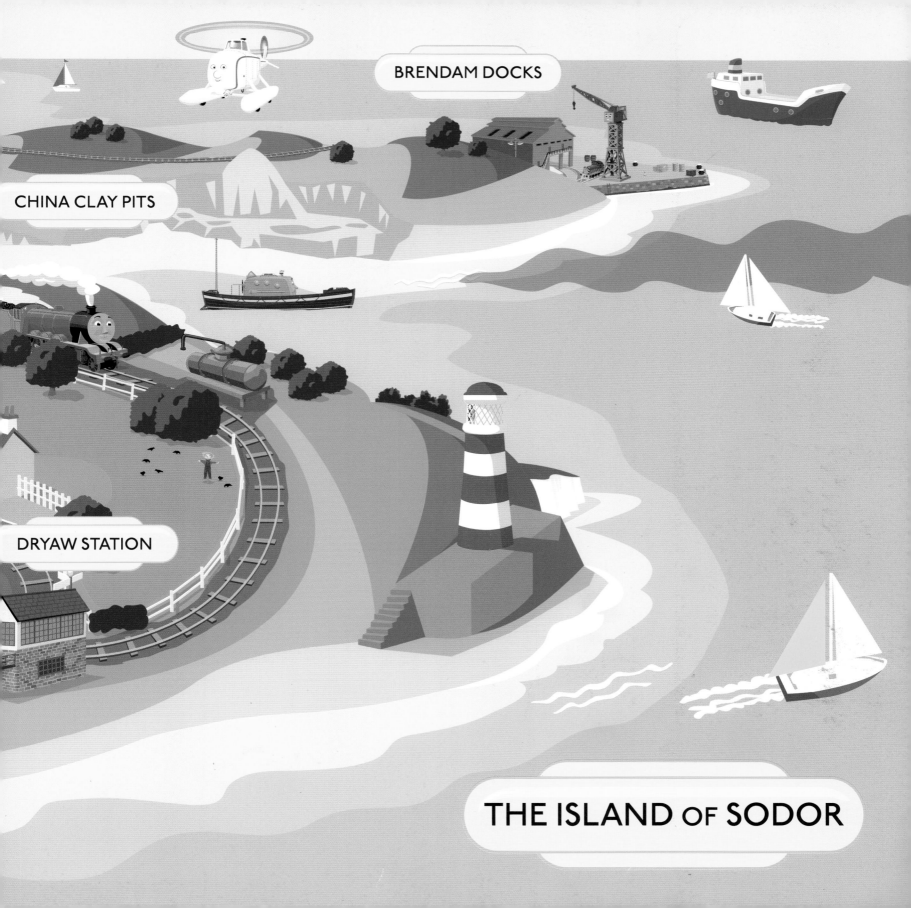

BRENDAM DOCKS

CHINA CLAY PITS

DRYAW STATION

THE ISLAND OF SODOR

About the creator

The Reverend W. Awdry was the creator of 26 little books about Thomas and his famous engine friends, the first being published in 1945. The stories came about when the Reverend's two-year-old son Christopher was ill in bed with the measles. Awdry invented stories to amuse him, which Christopher then asked to hear time and time again. And all these years later, children around the world continue to ask to hear these stories about Thomas, Edward, Gordon, James and the many other Really Useful Engines.

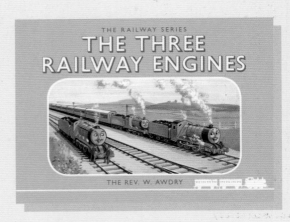

The Three Railway Engines, first published in 1945.

The Reverend Awdry with some of his readers at a model railway exhibition.